To Adam, our sweetheart,
with love, hugs and kisses from
Mum, Dad, Harry, Robbie and Molly.

Adam is an angel and lives on a cloud
and makes his Mummy and Daddy so proud.
With long golden hair you just could not miss,
he always has time for a hug and a kiss.
The message he sends from his cloud every day,
is to spend more time with each other and play.
The most important thing in life is this,
show your love for your family with a hug and a kiss.

Written by Benji Bennett.
benji@adamscloud.com

Illustrations by Roxanne Burchartz.
Roxanneburchartz@gmail.com

Designed by Bold.
www.reallybold.com

This 2013 edition printed in Ireland by Watermans Printers.
www.watermansprinters.ie

ISBN 978-1-906818-01-2

Published by

An imprint of Adam's Printing Press Publishing.

Adam's Cloud is dedicated to spreading Adam's message of the importance of love, laughter and play within the family and will make a donation from the proceeds of all books published under its imprint to children's charities.

Adam's Cloud
PO Box 11379, Blackrock, Co. Dublin, Ireland.
Email: info@adamscloud.com
Web: www.adamscloud.com
Tel: +353 1 2833620

2% of the proceeds from the sale of this book will go to

Make-A-Wish Foundation® International has approved this promotion and is very grateful to Adam's Printing Press for their support of our mission, which is to grant the wishes of children with life-threatening medical conditions to enrich the human experience with hope, strength and joy. For more information, please visit www.worldwish.org

I love you much more than the Sun, Moon and Stars,
even much more than the red planet Mars.
I love you much more than the outer space tune,
sung to the world by the man on the Moon.

Adam and Harry are astronaut men,
and fly around the earth again and again.
"Time for a trip in our space rocket ship,"
said Harry to Adam as a grin crossed his lip.
"That sounds cool, but where will we go,"
Adam replied, as the earth passed below.

"Out into space, to the moon and the stars,
and find out where aliens drive in their cars."
"Cool," said Adam then pulled out the choke,
and blasted off in a big cloud of smoke.
Then all of a sudden and ever so soon,
their space rocket ship arrived on the Moon.

"Hello, Mister Moon, and how do you do,
do aliens drive in their cars here with you?"
"No," the Moon said, "but it's not 'coz I'm grumpy,
it's simply because my ground is too bumpy.
The man on the moon is called Neil Armstrong,
when he flies around me he sings a love song.

"The song that he sings helps me to fly,
all the way round the starry night sky.
My advice to find cars is to visit the Sun,
he's the oldest in space and is why life begun."
"Thank you," said Adam, "we'll take your advice."
Then blasted off in his flying device.

"Hello, Mister Sun, and how do you do,
do aliens drive in their cars here with you?"
"Sorry," the Sun said, "but I'm afraid not,
it's mainly because my ground is too hot.
I'm in charge of the planets and shine really bright,
so children can play in the warmth of my light."

When I get tired and go down for the night,
that's when I sleep and turn off my light."
The Sun looked at the boys and their rocket with wings,
and said, "look for the planet with big shiny rings."
"Thanks very much for a very good clue."
The boys waved goodbye and away they flew.

"Hello, Mister Saturn, and how do you do,
do aliens drive in their cars here with you?"
"No," Saturn said, "but it's not 'coz I'm sad,
it's simply because the air here is bad.
When visitors visit they play on my swings,
I made them from chocolate and bits of my rings."
"Cool," said Adam, with a big shiny smile,
"do you mind if we stay here and play for a while?"

"Spend as long as you like," was Saturn's reply.
So they swung on his swings and slid down his slide.
Saturn said, "thank you for playing with me,
now fly to the biggest planet you see."
"Thanks very much for a very good clue."
The boys waved goodbye and away they flew.

Flying through space the boys felt in the mood,
to stop at an outer space diner for food.
They ate solar saussies with blue Brussels sprouts,
and asteroid nuggets fizzed up in their mouths.

Then back in his rocket just after his tea,
Adam could not believe what his brown eyes could see.
"Look, *Harry*, look!" he said with a shout,
"we've found the big planet, I'm sure, I've no doubt."

"Hello, Mister Jupiter, and how do you do,
do aliens drive in their cars here with you?"
"No," said Jupiter, "for years how I've tried,
but aliens think I'm too big and too wide.
I am so massive, so big and so strong,
to drive around me takes ever so long."

"Everyone knows about my big huge red spot,
inside it is windy and really quite hot.
To give you a clue I can think of just one,
visit the planet that's nearest the Sun."
"Thanks very much for a very good clue."
The boys waved goodbye and away they flew.

"Hello, Mister Mercury, and how do you do,
do aliens drive in their cars here with you?"
"No," said Mercury, "despite my promotion,
I'm so near the Sun they need too much sun lotion.
I'm the fastest in space and trail a hot blaze,
to fly round the Sun takes just 88 days."

"To see me from earth you must sharpen your eyes,
you can only see me at sunset and sunrise.
Take this advice on your tour of duty,
and look for the goddess of love and true beauty."
"Thanks very much for a very good clue."
The boys waved goodbye and away they flew.

"Hello, Lady Venus, and how do you do,
do aliens drive in their cars here with you?"
"Sorry, sweet Adam, but they're not allowed,
because I am covered with a fluffy white cloud.
After the Sun and the Moon way up high,
I'm the next brightest thing you can see in the sky.

You can see me from Earth as I shine really bright,
I'm the first star to twinkle at the start of each night.
To find your space cars, sweet Adam and Harry,
you must visit the old and wise comet Halley."
"Thanks very much for a very good clue."
The boys waved goodbye and away they flew.

Flying through space Adam had a sad face,
"we'll never find space cars on this wild goose chase."
Then all of a sudden way out in the dark,
Adam could see what looked like a spark.
"Hello, comet Halley, and how do you do,
do aliens drive in their cars here with you?"
"No," said Halley, who was ever so nice,
"they can't drive on me 'coz I'm made of cold ice.

I see everything as I travel quite far,
and can fly round the Sun and out past a star.
Sometimes I visit the blue planet Earth,
I even flew past on the day of your birth.
To find out where aliens drive in their cars,
you must go and visit the red planet Mars."
"Thanks very much for the very best clue."
The boys waved goodbye and away they flew.

"Yahoo," said Adam, as they flew through the stars,
"plot us a course for the red planet Mars."
"Aye, aye, Captain Adam," was Harry's reply,
and they arrived in what seemed like the blink of an eye.
"Hello Mister Mars, and how do you do,
do aliens drive in their cars here with you?"

"I heard you were coming, my astronaut friends,
and this is where your space mission ends.
All of the aliens that live out in space,
visit my planet to have a car race.
Harry and Adam had hours of fun,
playing with aliens under the Sun.

7
Finish

"Adam," said Harry, "this is such fun,
but it's way past our bed time and now we must run."
The aliens gave Adam a hug and a kiss,
and waved goodbye to friends they would miss.
With their mission complete the boys giggled and cheered,
and they flew towards Earth as red Mars disappeared.

They landed their spaceship by Dad's garden shed,
took off their space suits and jumped into bed.
Mum and Dad kissed the boys and turned off their light,
and the outer space astronauts slept all through the night.

It's time to sleep and wish on a star,
and dream of wonderful things both near and afar
My love for you is as bright as sunlight
sweet dreams, my love, I kiss you good night.